80 002 942 535

D0531547

Please return/renew this item by the last date
shown. Books may be renewed by
telephoning, writing to or calling in at any
library or on the Internet.

Northamptonshire Libraries and Information Service

**Northamptonshire
County Council**

www.northamptonshire.gov.uk/leisure/libraries/

This edition published 2008
First published 2001 by
A & C Black Publishers Ltd
38 Soho Square, London, W1D 3HB

www.acblack.com

Text copyright © 2001 Michael Hardcastle
Illustrations copyright © 2001 Bob Moulder
Cover illustration copyright © 2008 Anthony Williams

The rights of Michael Hardcastle and Bob Moulder to be
identified as author and illustrator of this work respectively
have been asserted by them in accordance with the
Copyrights, Designs and Patents Act 1988.

ISBN 978-0-7136-8638-8

A CIP catalogue for this book is available
from the British Library.

This book is produced using paper that is made from wood
grown in managed, sustainable forests. It is natural, renewable and
recyclable. The logging and manufacturing processes conform to
the environmental regulations of the country of origin.

Printed and bound in China by C&C Offset Printing.

Hit It!

Michael Hardcastle

illustrated by Bob Moulder

A & C Black • London

Chapter One

Leaning left and then right, sharply twisting right again and then left, Scott cut into the penalty area. As he avoided one opponent after another, the ball remained completely under his control.

He was sure he was going to score the goal that would move the Aces up the league.

And I'm going to pick up the trophy for being the Aces' top scorer this season.

No chance!

Kel grinned before charging after the ball. Scott and Kel had never been best friends off the pitch, but usually they weren't such deadly rivals on it.

Scott remained angry for the rest of the match, and that didn't help his play. He missed an easy chance to score, kicking the ball wide of the net. Luckily, the Aces didn't concede another goal. They won 2–1, to move nearer to the top of the league.

As the players changed after the match, Jed Royce, the Aces' coach, took Scott to one side.

You almost messed things up for us today, didn't you, Scott?

What's that supposed to mean?

You were too slow. If Kel hadn't moved fast, it could've been the opposition that took the ball off you. That red-haired defender was coming at you, but you weren't aware of him. Good thing Kel got there first.

Scott knew there was no point in arguing. The coach never really listened to any of his players. His own point of view was the only one that mattered to him.

Look, I know you've got a lot of skill, and I know being a bit short-sighted doesn't affect your game.

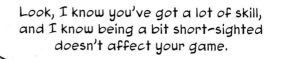

You've got great instincts for goal-scoring opportunities, you can beat defenders, and you can pass the ball like a rocket.

But, Scott lad, you're slow to react. You give up too easily. When you lose the ball, you don't fight to get it back.
Scott didn't speak, knowing it would be a waste of time. In any case, Coach Royce was more interested in defence than attack.
I want you on my team, but only if you improve your work ethic and show more fight.

And don't try to walk the ball into the net again. When you're in front of the goal, blast it in. Hit it as hard as you can! Learn from Kel. He always knows what to do.

That reminded Scott about what Kel had done.

Hey, he took the ball from me, scoring a goal that was mine! He had no right to do that, Coach.

Jed shook his head.

You're wrong there, lad. He had every right. He was thinking fast. He got the goal we needed.

I promise you this, Scott. If you move as fast as Kel to take the ball off him and hit it in the net, I'll be the happiest coach in the game.

For the rest of the day, Scott's family couldn't get a word out of him. All Scott could think about was Coach Royce's remarks. He wondered whether he would soon be off the team. The Aces were the best thing in his life. If he didn't play for them, he'd feel terrible.

Scott wanted to say yes, he was hurting badly. Instead, he shook his head.

Remember I told you my dad's fitness centre is opening soon?

Yeah.

It opens next week, but we can go there tonight, just the two of us. We can try out any of the equipment. So, how about it?

Hey, sounds good, Ali. Thanks! That would be great!

Ali's father had just retired from boxing. Running the fitness centre was his new career. Scott had never been inside one, so he was keen to see what it was like.

On the walls were posters advertising the fights that Harri Hosein had fought. He'd been a champion at his weight.

One in particular caught Scott's attention.

I never ran! Some of the sports writers said I was hard-hitting. I liked that. I tell you, nobody hit harder than I did. That's important. The harder you hit, the less of a chance your opponent has of staying with you.

Scott blinked. This was the second piece of advice he'd been given in a few hours about the value of hitting hard.

Why don't you have a go? See how good you are.

Harri demonstrated how to punch with rapid blows, skipping lightly on his toes as he did so.

Let's get you some gloves. Got to do this properly. Ali's already got his own pair, but we have some that will fit you.

It felt strange to have his hands taped inside the gloves.

Yeah, that'll do!

Scott was eager to start punching, but...

It's like hitting a concrete wall. I can't move it at all! I must be as weak as a kitten.

Look, son, you've got to put your whole body into it. You've got to use your shoulders.

That's where the power comes from.

It slowly began to get easier.

SMACK!

Hey!
It moved!
It moved!

All the same, Scott soon felt he'd never done anything so tiring in his life. He was glad when it was Ali's turn. Of course, his friend had done this before, and Scott was impressed by the speed of his punches.

POW!

Ali could also manage to hit the same area. Scott's punches had landed all over the place.

OK, time!

How do you feel about that, Scott?

Great!

Scott had found his second bout of punching just as tough as the first, but he wasn't going to admit it.

I don't think I'm as fit as you need to be for boxing.

Well, come back and have another go whenever you want. You'll always be welcome, won't he, Ali?

Of course.

Then, a few minutes later, they were all speeding back home in Mr Hosein's sports car. Scott was aching in muscles he never knew he had, but he still felt he'd achieved something at the fitness centre.

29

After Kel had finished in a slightly faster time, he came over to Scott.

Got a new hobby?

What's that supposed to mean?

Well, I hear you like boxing, but I bet you can't punch your way out of a paper bag!

Rubbish! Where did you hear about that?

Scott knew Ali hadn't been talking to Kel. They didn't even know each other. So how had Kel found out?

33

It turned out to be a game of head tennis. Although Scott was one of the shorter players, he had good spring in his legs and could jump higher than many of the others.

In spite of his height advantage, Kel wasn't very accurate with his headers.

On one occasion, he missed the ball completely.

That was rubbish, Kel.

I just got some mud in my eye. I can't see a thing.

Mud? The pitch is bone dry!

They didn't have a practice game, and Scott wasn't able to show Coach Royce how fast he could react to things on the field. Scott was worried that the coach would drop him before he had a chance to prove he could score whenever he was in sight of the goal.

They planned that Scott would visit Kel's house the following Saturday morning.

He'll be at his fiercest. He seems to know it's the weekend and he can do what he wants – like eat a few people!

Don't worry, I'll be there. He won't even growl at me.

Scott always got on well with animals and never felt afraid of them. Somehow, they seemed to sense he cared for them.

As a small boy, he'd decided he wanted to be a vet and hadn't changed his mind. After all, he could still play football in his spare time. However, he knew how aggressive a Rottweiler could be. So he took some dog treats with him just in case.

Chapter Four

When he arrived, Kel's mum answered the door.

Hello, Mrs Kellerman. I've come to see the dog.

I wouldn't if I were you.

It's a crazy animal. You should stay away from it. Don't say I didn't warn you, Scott.

For the first time, Scott felt a little nervous. If Kel's mum worried about the Rottweiler, then it might be wilder than he'd imagined.

Kel was rubbing his hands with delight.

He's got a cage at the bottom of the garden.

You're in for a treat. Hope you're ready!

Frenzied barking started the moment the animal sensed a stranger was present. Kel was already talking to the dog as they approached the cage, but it made no difference.

Billy's frantic barking stopped completely. There weren't any growls, and the hair on his coat was flat. All his aggression seemed to have vanished. He looked as if he was listening to their conversation.

Listen, I'm going to let him out now, but I'll keep him on the leash because he'll probably try to attack you.

Seems a bit quiet today, though. Hope he's not ill again.

Scott said nothing as Billy was taken out of the cage.

45

Scott said he had to leave.

I'm really glad you came over. If ever I can do something for you, I will.

But I'm still going to finish the season as the Aces' top scorer. I won't let you take that away from me, Scott.

Oh, we'll see about that.

Chapter Five

When Scott got off the treadmill at the fitness centre, Ali was waiting for him.

How do you feel now? You look exhausted.

No, I'm not. I'm building up my stamina. Never felt fitter.

If you don't push yourself, you're not training properly. Your dad told me that.

OK, if you say so.

Scott wanted to be in top form for the Aces' away game at Weather Hill, one of the league's worst teams. Scott saw it as a chance to increase his goal total and catch up with Kel. Kel was worried because he hurt his ankle during practice. Coach Royce had lined up a replacement, Warren, in case Kel couldn't play. Warren had never played a full game for them so far and had only been a sub a couple of times.

The sky looked dark and stormy, with heavy rain and a strong wind. Weather Hill was living up to its name.

I suppose the locals are used to this weather, but I don't like it. The ball's always harder to control when it's wet.

You just have to get used to it, Warren. It's the same for both sides.

Scott changed. He was feeling good about the game. He'd been training hard and thought his new fitness routine was paying off.

Then, just as Coach Royce was beginning his last-minute team talk, Kel burst in.

Sorry I'm late, Coach. Had to go to the chemist to pick up my mum's medicine.

With an explanation like that, the coach couldn't blame his leading scorer for being late.

Just get changed, son, quick as you can. Warren, you'll be on the bench now.

Warren didn't look too unhappy.

Hey, those tablets for Billy are fantastic! He's like a new dog. Fiercer than ever. I owe you one. I brought Billy to the game. A friend of mine's looking afer him.

Scott smiled. He was glad to hear about Billy's health, but disappointed that Kel would get the chance to add to his goal total after all. And Kel was in the best of moods.

Weather Hill didn't begin like a weak side. They were fast, eager and physical. Scott was tripped the first time he had the ball.

Hey, watch it!

Better get used to it.

Scott wasn't hurt, but he vowed he wouldn't let that player get near him again.

The rain was making the field very slippery, but Scott could cope with that. His speed and quick changes of direction left many opponents in despair. One of his passes set Kel up.

But Kel blasted the ball wildly over the bar.

Scott got the impression that Kel wasn't really fit enough to be playing. When his tall team-mate went down under a brutal tackle, he needed to have his ankle taped before he could hobble back into the game.

Then Kel was fouled on the edge of the box. The free kick was taken quickly, and the Weather Hill defence was caught napping.

Kel was free. He rounded the goalkeeper...

...and an open goal lay before him.

That's the one I owed you. Just don't expect another!

So the Aces won 1–0 to keep up their promotion challenge. If they hadn't, Jed told Kel, he would never have forgiven him. Kel wasn't really listening. His ankle injury had flared up again.

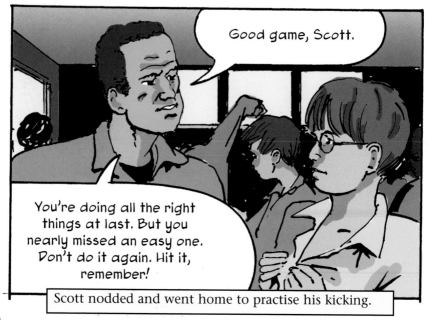

Good game, Scott.

You're doing all the right things at last. But you nearly missed an easy one. Don't do it again. Hit it, remember!

Scott nodded and went home to practise his kicking.

Chapter Six

At the last game of the season, the Aces needed just one point for promotion. Kel was the team's top scorer. Scott was one goal behind him.

Kel still hadn't fully recovered from his ankle injury and had missed two games. Scott, his confidence increasing game by game, believed he could still snatch the trophy as the team's top goal scorer.

Look, what we need here is an early goal.
Then we can sit on our lead for the rest of the game.
Make sure we get at least a draw out of it.

As usual, defence dominated Coach Royce's thinking.

Kel was testing the
strapping on his ankle.

If I can get six goals,
I will. One goal's
never enough.

The Lions, their opponents, were not a strong team, but they still wanted to finish the season on a winning note. They started with a rush and pinned the Aces in their own half.

Twice the Lions almost got the ball in the net because of a nervous defence.

Jed was getting redder in the face by the second.

Scott got the chance when the defence cleared the ball, and he picked it up in midfield. For, as he ran at them, one opponent slipped on the soft ground, and another missed a tackle completely.

…and Kel kicked it in!

Ali stood on the sideline, cheering.

It was hard to tell who was happier, Jed or Kel. Scott was happy for both of them. He knew now he had no real chance of winning the goal-scoring trophy, even though minutes later Kel limped off after another fierce knock on his ankle. The coach reorganised the team defensively, and Scott was ordered to stay back.

With the Aces' players staying back, the Lions were able to attack. Scott was running a lot, but not enjoying it. His game was all about attacking, and that wasn't allowed...

...not even when, in the second half, the Lions scored.

With the game tied, the Aces had the point they needed to win the league championship. But they were in danger of losing because the Lions kept attacking.

Then a Lions player miskicked badly. The ball ballooned into the air before spinning backwards towards the Lions' goal.

He was almost there, when a tackle
from behind brought him down.

It was outside the penalty area. Direct free kick.

The Lions quickly formed a defensive wall, but the Aces players were in no hurry.

What should we do?

Waste as much time as possible. The ref will call time soon.

Scott had other ideas.

This is mine!

He placed the ball and looked at the wall that had formed in front of him.

The ball sailed through the space like a rocket. The Lions' goalie didn't even see it as it went past him and lifted the net.

It was the goal that clinched the
game and the Aces' promotion.